Lorraine Carey

illustrated by
Migy Blanco

Text copyright © 2015 by Lorraine Carey
Illustrations copyright © 2015 by Migy Blanco

Nosy Crow and its logos are trademarks of Nosy Crow, Ltd. Used under license.

First U.S. edition 2015

Library of Congress Catalog Card Number 2014951804
ISBN 978-0-7636-8005-3

15 16 17 18 19 20 GBL 10 9 8 7 6 5 4 3 2 1

Printed in Shenzhen, Guangdong, China

This book was typeset in Cochin.
The illustrations were created digitally.

Nosy Crow
an imprint of
Candlewick Press
99 Dover Street
Somerville, Massachusetts 02144

www.nosycrow.com
www.candlewick.com

Cinderella's Stepsister
and the
BIG BAD
WOLF

nosy crow™

An imprint of Candlewick Press

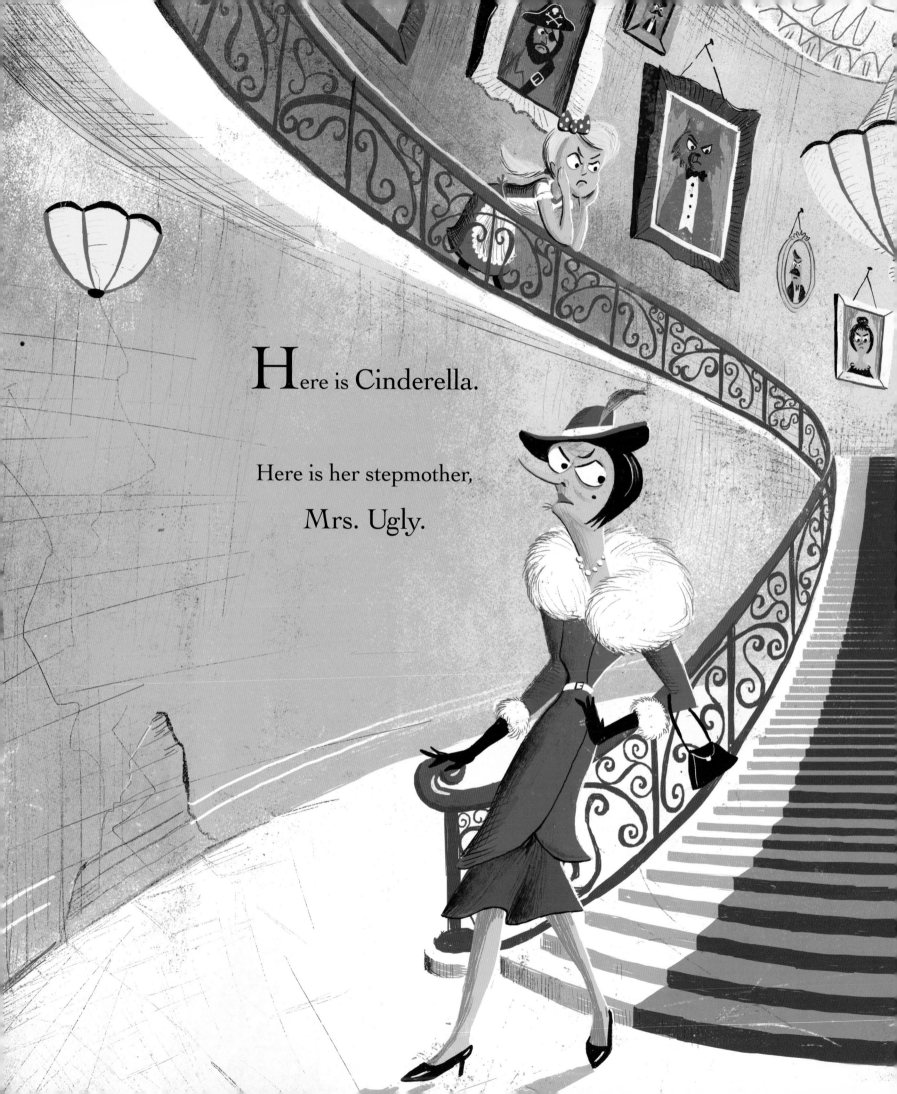

Here is Cinderella.

Here is her stepmother,

Mrs. Ugly.

Here are the Ugly sisters:

one, two, and . . .

three.

You already know the two Ugly sisters

who were horrible, nasty, and mean.

But Gertie, their little sister, was . . . nice.

While Cinderella lazed about and did absolutely **nothing**, Gertie watered the pumpkins, took care of the mice, and did **all** the housework.

Niceness shone from Gertie's face, and her smile was **brighter** than the sun.

Well, of course,

the Ugly family despaired.

They were **ashamed**.

They hid little Gertie away,

and they never let her go **anywhere** with them.

Then, one morning, a special invitation arrived.

"Oooh, look!"
said Mrs. Ugly.
"We're invited to a
grand ball at the
palace tonight!"

"A ball?" cried Gertie. "Oh, please, can I go?"

"You?" said Mrs. Ugly. "Go to the ball?
You're a disgrace to the Ugly name.
You don't walk Ugly, you don't talk Ugly,
and with that shocking smile on your face,
you don't even look Ugly!"

"But I am an Ugly sister," Gertie said,
"and I can be bad—I know I can!"

"You'll need help,"
said Mrs. Ugly.
"A lesson from the Wicked Queen
should do the trick!"

So that afternoon
Gertie was sent to learn
from the Wicked Queen,
who was just about to visit
Snow White . . . with a poisoned apple.

First the Wicked Queen disguised herself as a little old lady.

Then she knocked on the door.

"Hello, my dear," she said to Snow White.

"Won't you take a bite of this **lovely** apple?"

"Look out, Snow White!"
Gertie shouted.
"That apple is poisoned!"
"No thanks, then,"
said Snow White.
And she shut the door.

Well, the Wicked Queen was furious
and sent Gertie home faster than a streak of lightning.
Mrs. Ugly was very angry, but Gertie begged
for another chance. "Oh, all right!" said Mrs. Ugly.
"But this time you're going to see the Worst Witch of all. . . ."

"Being bad is **easy**," said the Worst Witch.

"Let me show you how.

The oven's nice and hot,

and I'm planning a

delicious dinner!

Hansel! Gretel!

Come in, children!"

Gertie tried hard but she just couldn't keep quiet.
"Don't come in!" she yelled.
"The witch is planning to eat
YOU for dinner!"

"In that case, we won't be staying,"

said Hansel and Gretel.

"But we'll take some snacks with us."

Back home, Mrs. Ugly was furious.

"Oh, please!" Gertie wailed. "Please let me go to the ball!

I can be mean and bad like a real Ugly sister. I know I can!"

And she cried so much that Mrs. Ugly

agreed to give her one last chance. But this time,

Gertie was sent to the meanest and nastiest villain of all . . .

the big bad Wolf—

who happened to be wearing a dress!

"So, you wanna be Ugly, huh?"

said the Wolf.

"You wanna be BAD?"

"Oh, I do!" said Gertie.
"I do! I do!"

"Well," said the Wolf,
"you're just in time! Watch this!"

Suddenly,
there was a
knock, knock, knock on the door.

Little Red Riding Hood skipped in.

"Oh, Grandma," said Little Red Riding Hood, "what big eyes you have."

"All the better to see you with," said the Wolf.

"Oh, Grandma," said Little Red Riding Hood, "what big ears you have."

"All the better to hear you with," said the Wolf.

"Oh, Grandma," said Little Red Riding Hood, "what big teeth—"

"Stop!" Gertie shouted.

"That's not your grandma, that's . . .

the big bad Wolf!"

And Little Red Riding Hood scampered off.

The Wolf turned to Gertie and drooled.

"Please don't eat me!" said Gertie. "I've tried so hard to be mean and bad like the rest of my family so I could go to the ball, and—"

"Ball?" said the Wolf. "Did you just say . . . ball? I've always wanted to go to a ball!"

"Come on," said Gertie. "Let's see what we can do!"

By the time Gertie and the Wolf arrived home, Mrs. Ugly and the two Ugly sisters had already left for the ball. "We're too late!" cried Gertie, when who should appear but a beautiful fairy!

"I am your Fairy Godmother!" she said. She looked at Gertie and the Wolf. "And I expect you two want to go to the ball, don't you?"

"Stop!" shouted an angry voice.

It was **Cinderella**.
"What about me?"
she screeched.
"I've been waiting **all** night
for a Fairy Godmother
to get **me** to that ball!"

Well, Fairy Godmothers
do **not** like bad manners,
so she quickly
turned Cinderella
into a . . .

mouse.

But Gertie and the Wolf went to the ball in beautiful new dresses.

And they had a **lovely** time.

So lovely, in fact, that Gertie and Prince Charming

fell in love and married soon after.

As for Mrs. Ugly and Gertie's
two Ugly sisters . . .

well, no one quite knows

why, but they were never, ever . . .

seen again.